TINKLE'S MOUTH
An Existential Comic Diary

TINA'S MOUTH

An Existential Comic Diary

KESHNI KASHYAP

Illustrated by
MARI ARAKI

For information about permission to reproduce selections from this book,
write to Permissions, Houghton Mifflin Harcourt Publishing Company,
215 Park Avenue South, New York, New York 10003.

www.hmhbooks.com

Library of Congress Cataloging-in-Publication Data

Kashyap, Keshni.
Tina's mouth : an existential comic diary / Keshni Kashyap ;
illustrated by Mari Araki.
    p. cm.
Summary: Tina Malhotra, a sophomore at the Yarborough Academy in Southern
California, creates an existential diary for an honors English assignment in
which she tries to determine who she is and where she fits in.
  ISBN 978-0-618-94519-1
[1. Graphic novels. 2. Individuality—Fiction. 3. East Indian Americans—Fiction.
4. High schools—Fiction. 5. Schools—Fiction. 6. California, Southern—Fiction.]
I. Araki, Mari, ill. II. Title.
  PZ7.7.K38Ti 2012
  741.5'973—dc23   2011030439

Book design by Bethany Powell
Printed in the United States of America
DOC 10 9 8 7 6 5 4 3 2 1

The day is coming when I fly off,
but who is it now in my ear who hears my voice?
Who says words with my mouth?

— Jelaluddin Rumi

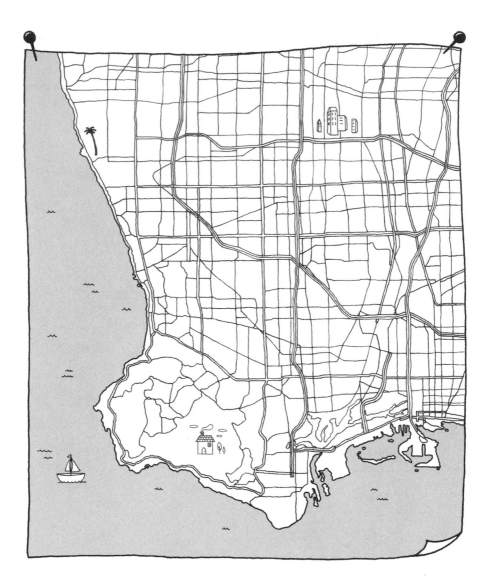

January 26

Dear Mr. Jean-Paul Sartre,

I know that you are dead and old and also a philosopher. So, on an obvious level, you and I do not have a lot in common.

I live in a place that is a little bit like France in that we have cliffs and waves and temperate weather. We also have things like surfers and pot and a thoroughly disgusting beverage called Jägermeister that people drink to escape the understanding of their existence, something I believe is your area of expertise.

I'm not one of those girls who write in diaries about boys and popularity and that sort of thing, in case you were wondering. This diary is strictly a class project for my English Honors elective in existential philosophy, taught by Mr. Moosewood — AKA Moose — who supposedly smokes pot, which makes him the most popular teacher at school. We've each been assigned a semester project, the whole point being to figure out who you are and who you are becoming. Moose has been doling out some juicy options such as examining your garbage every day or making videotapes of the contents of your fridge. It's the sort of new-age malarkey teachers at my school are into.

But most people are choosing to do an existential diary such as this. At the end of the semester, the diary will be sealed and given to Moose. He won't read it, but will mail it back to me after three full years. I've got some business that needs sorting out and the whole writing-it-all-down bit could be useful. As for you, I like your face and your wandering eye, which makes you seem as if you were looking in two directions at once....

ENGLISH 1 HONORS:
Existentialism Semester Project

January 26

Who Am I, Really?

My name is Tina.

I am fifteen years old and I go to a school called Yarborough Academy. The name makes it sound fancier than all the public schools in the area. You'd really think the Prince of Wales attended. But it's just a boring school started by some guy who died eons ago. I've been going here since third grade.

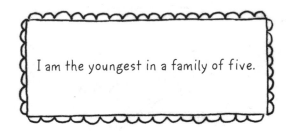

I am the youngest in a family of five.

Daddy

These are my parents —
my dad, Dr. Deepak Malhotra,
and my mom, Leena.

Dr. Deepak Malhotra
A Cardiologist

They got married thirty years ago by my grandmother's doing and then they left Bombay, India

The Times of INDIA

13

This is my sister, Anjali, who is 24. She graduated from Columbia with a degree in Architecture. She doesn't know what she wants to do and moved home to "figure things out," a phrase that is not entirely understood by my father. Anjali has strong opinions about everything.

She's also an artist and was part of a show in New York City. Her painting was called "Bodies."

My mom and dad and I went to New York to see it. I didn't get it, but everyone else seemed to think it was awesome.

This is my brother, Rahul, who is 28. He's in medical school and lives in San Diego, where he's studying to be a cardio-something surgeon. He's what you might call a square.

(Okay. Maybe a pentagon.)

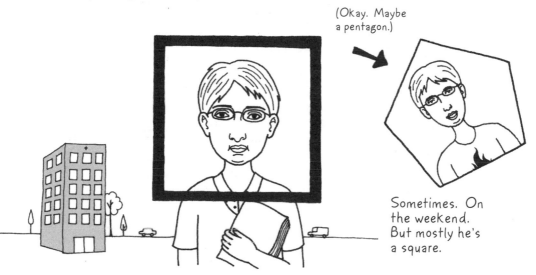

Sometimes. On the weekend. But mostly he's a square.

He's trying to find a girlfriend, or at least that's what my mom says. So he joined an Indian dating website called SuitableAlliance.com, where his undergraduate education at Stanford is a pretty well-received detail.

100 matches for you!!!!!

And this is Alex...who has a beautiful voice and sings like a bird.

She's been my best friend since fourth grade.

She's also Mormon, but ever since her parents split, she's turned into this big potty mouth.

Have you ever thought about anal sex? Do you think it hurts?

As for me, I don't talk too much. But...

I'm a pretty good student.

A decent violin player.

And a bit of an intellectual.

B+

SIX PISTOLS

BETTY FRIEDAN

However, the question I get asked the most is:

Now I know this is a generalization, but there are usually two responses:

But really now....

MEDITATE? Do you meditate? Do you

BOLLYWOOD Why do BOLLYWOOD

Can you movies have so much singing

HAVE A DOWRY?

COW

LEVITATE? Do YOU HAVE A GURU? ARE YOU GOING TO NIRVANA. Tell me about

and dancing?

....What's UP with the BLUE GOD? Why is the

This got me thinking.

Here at Yarborough, things are very divided.

There are sixty people in our class and everyone seems to have their own group. 1. The partiers, 2. The surfers, 3. The waterpolo players, 4. The freakazoid people, 5. The intellectual types, 6. The hippies, 7. The cheerleaders (who because this is a prep school are short, fat, and out of sync), 8. The comic heads and Mensa people, 9. The skaters, 10. The rock climbers, 11. The band people, chorus people, and the drama geeks, who generally are lumped together.

The question of **who I am,** the purpose of this diary, is a worthy question.

But I don't know if I **care** that much.

The truth is that there is something else on my mind. It's something I think about a lot.

It's my mouth.

Mouths are underrated. They speak, they taste, they sing. They make noise and quiet. They are portals. That's one of my favorite SAT words.

And they do "other things." Or so I'm told. ♥

But there is one most important thing that a mouth does:

It kisses.

Which brings me to the real thing that I think about. The truth, all truth, nothing but the TRUTH.

I want to kiss someone... →

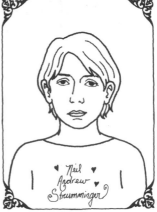

And there is only one person in the world who I want to kiss who I've wanted to kiss for an entire year. His name is Neil Andrew Strumminger.

Who knows why people fall in love. They just do. Maybe he looks like somebody from a past life that I was in love with.

Or maybe it was that day when we were alone in the photo studio and he was breathing on my shoulder and he was kind of embarrassed because the picture he was developing was of his grandmother while everyone else took photos of skateboarders or pets or stupid pictures on the boardwalk in Redondo. And then my picture showed up and it was **my** grandmother!

That's far-out that we both took pictures of our grandmas!

Yeah!

Plus he's the most popular guy at Yarborough. Known to be nice, charming, and an excellent skater. His locker is next to mine and sometimes he says hi to me.

There is, however, a much bigger problem. His girlfriend: Ava Petropoulos.

She's the daughter of this sporting-goods magnate and he just bought her a Porsche in a shade that matches the color of her eyes.

For some people, finding someone is so easy. For others, they have to wait and wait and wait to even have their first kiss.

To be honest, Sartre, up until last week...

...I did not have the slightest interest in the meaning of my existence.

Last week, however, a **really annoying event** occurred that actually makes me wonder about you and some of the stuff you say.

* ✿ I like you, Sartre, so I clipped your face out of the reader. And taped it to the wall above my bed where I keep a photo of my grandmother and other interesting artifacts.

What **really annoying event**, you ask?

✳ Let me start at the beginning....

In fourth grade, my friend Alex moved to California from Salt Lake City. It was just after the summer I had developed a crush on Krishna.

On the first day of school, I brought along a drawing of him to show my friends. Everyone thought it was weird and strange except for Alex...

Weird!

Haha!

Looks like a girl!

I love him, too!

...who felt his blue color went well with my own olive hue. We became best friends that day. And school became a better place.

As I grew, my crush on Krishna faded and was replaced by more quotidian interests.

Eric Lim
(Sixth grade)

David Feldman
(Seventh grade)

Nick Abernathy
(Eighth grade)

But my crushes are always from afar. Alex, of course, had crushes too, but seldom from afar. Last year, she was caught making out with a Samoan convert named Edward by the church dumpster during a dance. Strictly against church rules.

WHAP
MMMPH
SMACK

DSM-V

Her dad, who's a shrink, got really mad and forbade her from ever attending again. So, in retaliation, we stole his DSM manual. It was an excellent bit of thieving because we have become a fine pair of experts.

Among other things, we have determined that:

Ted Fresh has an anti-social personality disorder

Katie Milanova is paranoid.

And Ava is a narcissist!

Sixth tube this month

Fuck you, you fucking fuck-head.

Are you talking about me?

More recently, with the help of Alex's older brother, James, who often functions as our chaperone and driver, we hang out at Trotsky's Grand Russian Buffet in downtown L.A., where we eat ghoulash and listen to musical acts from all over the world.

During community service last year, Mr. Spencer this crazy old man who lives at the convalescent home we volunteer at — muttered something dirty and racist. And do you know what Alex said?

Simon Lee, who was also there, made a T-shirt out of it and tried to sell it to everyone.

My grandmother used to tell me about the caste system in India and once I even did a presentation about it. Everyone thought it was totally barbaric, but high school is no different.

That's why I love Alex. We've never belonged to a clique. Any day, I'd prefer to be a clique of two.

We are different and the same.

And we have been this way forever.

However...

One year ago, Alex's parents, Dr. and Mrs. Leach, got a divorce. After the divorce, Mrs. Leach left the church. Which was a big deal because Alex went to live with her.

This is when I started to notice a series of shifts in Alex. Here are a few:

1. The wearing of super-tight clothes.

2. The rageful playing of music.

3. And the open flirtation with the skanky French teacher M. Suchet.

Hi!

Alex, Rachmaninoff should be played with restraint!

M. Suchet! Vous ressemblez beaucoup Serge Gainsbourg!

There was the unbridled admiration of Claudia Kidman, a self-obsessed clotheshorse.

I like your shoes!

?

But the biggest change happened when the chorus teacher cast a senior named Eric Weissman in a guitar solo with Alex during the Christmas concert.

And Alex fell in love.

This changed everything for me because lunch was no longer the two of us. And Alex and I never talked because she was always so engrossed in Eric. In fact, everyone was engrossed in everyone else.

So, as of November, we were no longer separatists. We had become firmly integrated into a group of pseudo-intellectual-future-art-school hipsters consisting of Claudia and her minions, including her boyfriend, Garrett, and all they do is sit around discussing clothes and bands and their poetry collections. And every day, Garrett brings out his guitar and plays with fervor while Eric chimes in and Claudia and Alex watch like a couple of starry-eyed DONKEYS.

And now it's **January** ...

...And **nothing's** changed except that the few conversations I have with Alex have turned into a long list of Eric this and Eric that.

HE's so funny
HE's got so much style
HE's so amazing
HE's so talented!
HE's a great kisser!

Until yesterday, when things came to a head.

It was the end of the day, and I was walking past the parking lot when I heard Mrs. Leach's voice.

Because I wasn't invited. The answer was obviously "no." Mrs. Leach awkwardly hemmed and hawed and said it was just an oversight and that she would talk to Alex.

But this was no oversight. Someone's mother cannot invite you to a party you're not wanted at.

I hadn't even spoken to Alex in days. I knew the truth and I couldn't ignore this anymore. So I waited for that rare moment when she was without Claudia or Eric. Which was basically never.

And I approached her....

Alex!

We walked to a secluded bench.

And that's when we had our fight.

Only it wasn't really a fight.

It was a lecture.

And so, with a cold "good luck," Alex Imogene Leach **deserted** me for Claudia, a flaky, bespectacled mannequin, and a new group of friends with whom she could discuss slutty clothes and cheesy poetry.

But she didn't. She flat-up ended our friendship. It sucked.

And this is where my story begins.

Yarborough Academy
K-12

ENGLISH 1 HONORS:
Existentialism Semester Project

February 2

Death Is Final and Random

Dear Jean-Paul Sartre,

If man is what he wills himself to be, as you say, then I — Tina M. — say this: it is impossible to be free when you are constantly being thwarted by an authoritarian regime.

The P.A.E., as it turns out, involves not just eating alone and doing homework alone, it also means having no reasonable excuse to escape family weekend activities (though my sister escaped, saying she had some art colony application due. A laughable excuse, bought hook, line, and sinker by my parents, who think that an art colony application is actual "work" and fail to see the bong she has hidden in her closet).

Anyway, there I was sitting in the car on Saturday evening wearing ill-fitting Indian clothes of three fashion seasons ago when I came up with three crystalline points.

1. There is no point to anything. 2. Because death is final and random. 3. And existentialism is brilliant.

Ah, Nisha.

Sulkiness really was the only antidote for this sorry excuse of a Saturday night.

Nisha is the daughter of Karishma Auntie and Mahesh Uncle. The last time we met, it was her great aspiration to be a "modelslashactressslashr&bsinger."

Mahesh Uncle and my dad have been golfing partners for a very long time. However, eight years ago, Mahesh Uncle became very very rich. In fact, even though they still send Nisha to public school, they're probably the richest people my parents know.

The reason for all this wealth was...

Not a **potato** chip, as I'd originally thought. But a **computer** chip. The chip changed everything. So they built:

The House

Which was distinguished by 1. a winding staircase in the front foyer, custom made for Bollywood-style descending, 2. tacky pieces of art like statues of white people doing ballet and kissing, 3. a ton of marble, and 4. a four-car garage left open for this and every party.

1

2

3

4

And don't forget Nisha's brother Ravi, who is in college and wants to be a hip-hop producer. He's the only Indian guy I know who has cornrows.

Before the chip, Nisha's family wasn't very rich at all, which is why my dad says that Mahesh Uncle is totally self-made. My mom says he has the worst taste ever.

You've outdone the Vatican.

That's just what I like to hear!

?

Tina, are you ready to get down and PARTY!?!

Even here things are pretty divided. Except that the breakdown is different. The aunties hang out with the aunties and the uncles hang out with the uncles. Tonight, in the living room, there was 1. Rima Auntie (So-Cool Auntie), 2. Mira Auntie (Nosy Auntie), 3. Sabina Auntie (Bling Auntie), 4. Bela Auntie (Snobby Auntie), and 5. Pinky Auntie, who my sister and I call Hook-Dat-Shit-Up Auntie for her superhuman matchmaking abilities. Pinky Auntie is one of my mom's best friends.

Closer to outside was where the uncles were hanging out. Tonight there was 1. Tejpal Uncle (Stock-Tips Uncle), 2. Prem Uncle (Sporty Uncle), 3. RJ Uncle (Party-All-Night Uncle), and 4. Bob Uncle (Hit-On-Every-Sixteen-Year-Old-With-Breasts Uncle, according to my sister).

On an average cultural Saturday night, all the kids my age hang out in the video room. So that's where we were headed. Which was fine. Except that now that Mahesh Uncle had this freaking mansion it meant that the hallway to the video room was half a mile long. This gave Nisha all the time in the world to talk about herself, which she does **insanely** well.

The fact of the matter is, I don't have a huge problem with Nisha. She's not a bad person as far as friendliness is concerned. She is just one huge **salesperson** about her life and that part is totally annoying. She recently got into "Seven Bells," this WASPy debutante society. I've seen photos of them in the Yarborough yearbook, and they're probably the last bastion of racial segregation in America. It must have been Karishma Auntie's idea. Ever since they became rich, she's become quite the social climber, if you want to know the truth. At least that's what my mom says.

Nauseating. What year is this? 1954? I mean, does anyone talk about anything other than boys?

We went to the video game room and Nisha played Jurassic Double Hijack while the boys salivated all over her....

...until Ravi came in and messed up her game.

Let me first **say**...

...Sartre, that a document such as this would be incomplete without addressing "mon existence Indienne."

Just so you know, my parents have never tried to lock me into a child marriage, nor have they pushed me into spelling competitions. All they really do is hang out every weekend with other Indians, and they want me to hang out with other Indians, which I don't mind except that I have **nothing** in common with Ravi and Nisha. I have more in common with Jassie, though that might be because he says about three words:

I would have happily spent the evening playing video games, but my mom is dead set against them and she keeps an eagle eye on me at these parties. It was only a matter of time before she started poking around the halls. As for my dad, he can't get enough of dancing.

I, for one, am not bad on the dance floor. I was tearing it up, in fact.

My parents complain about Mahesh Uncle and all his bad taste, but I could barely drag them away from the party.

A socialite in the making is what Nisha is. That's what I think.

Indeed, there is no harm done in being a good sport.

ENGLISH 1 HONORS:
Existentialism Semester Project

February 9

It's a Nice Day Out

Well, Sartre,

I have christened my spot behind the elementary school my "bench of existential solitude" and it is from this perch that I intend to examine all of life's unique questions.

Death is final and random?

I have no one to talk to anyway. That is, until this week came to a close.

It had been two weeks since the fight, and I was sitting on said bench eating lunch, tearing through a few more philosophical tomes. That's when Mr. Moosewood himself came up to me from behind. Because Mr. Moosewood has only been at Yarborough for a couple of years he doesn't go on and on about how brilliant my brother and sister were — the point being that I'm not, and I'm grateful for that. He does, however, constantly hit me up for conversations about India. He just loves India. He could go on about it forever.

Have I told you about this **blazing** experience I had out in Varanasi with Maharishi blah blah blah...

Anyway, I bring up Mr. Moosewood because that day, while I was sitting on my bench of existential solitude, minding my own business and doing my homework, he came up to me and said something that was **classic.**

I feel sad vibes from you.

Huh?

The teachers at Yarborough are really in your business.

So, Moose went on in his sensitivity-training sort of way, asking me if I was okay and this and that. It turns out that this was all small talk and what he really wanted was for me to try out for the spring play, which he was directing.

Now, the drama department at Yarborough is well-known for its ambitious productions.

Mostly pretentious bores — as you can see — existing solely for the drama geeks and their parents to freak out over, but I had a feeling that Moose's play was going to be cool.

I must admit, I was a bit flattered.

Moose may seem all spacy and vague, but he knows more than he lets on. He was right. I was spending way too much time alone. So the very next Monday, I ventured out and picked another bench. This time in a more public place...

...next to Su Ming, who was in my chemistry class.

I've always liked Su Ming, but I don't know her that well. She usually practices piano at lunch, but last week she sprained her wrist. So for the past few days, we two loners have been eating lunch together. I always thought she was really shy....

Jimi Hendrix blah, blah, blah, blah, Patti Smith, blah, blah, this blah, Talking Heads, blah.

You really have an encyclopedic knowledge of American popular culture.

But there is more to Su Ming than meets the eye. Neither of us seemed to have talked to anyone in a long time. And that was nice. Because Alex and Claudia were becoming the best of friends. Freaking twinning it out. Yesterday, in the hall, they were piggy-backing each other. They thought it was **so** funny.

Ha! Ha!

Ha! Ha!

So, Mr. Jean-Paul Sartre...

...I have decided to take Mr. Moosewood's advice and **curtail my existential solitude** by getting really really busy.

The first thing I did was that I went ahead and tried out for the play... I even got Su Ming to do it.

Hmmm...It's called Rashomon.

I hope it's good.

RASHOMON
By ____
Based on ____

Then I got ahead on my school assignments.

scribble scribble

Want to do the chem homework?

I already did it.

I got involved in more extracurriculars like Colin and Kalil's brown people club.

Dreadlocks are traditionally a symbol of ethnic pride and the rejection of mainstream establishment culture. We should be allowed to wear them if we want.

Jah love, baby.

Fight the power!

Yeah!

I also took on extra articles for the school newspaper, the YA **Herald** which is run by Noah — an active Republican party member with early acceptance to Princeton — and Susan — an active Green party member also with early acceptance to Princeton. Last week alone, I wrote articles on Mr. Grunbaum's eco-garden, the new gym, and how the homeless count in beach cities is growing.

Yet **another** article on homeless people?

Oh **god**, Noah. The slightest hair of social responsibility and we're all **flaaaaaming** liberals!

Sometimes during newspaper elective, I hang out with our family friend, Reza.

Reza is very quiet, but when you start talking to him, you realize he has a lot to say. His family left Iran and moved to the U.S., but when they came to America, Reza's father suddenly left his mother. His mom sometimes goes to Indian parties. According to my mom, she always seems a little sad. The one thing that makes her happy is talking about Reza.

I like Reza, even though he's kind of dorky. We have highly intellectual conversations.

You see how it is, Sartre?
We are intellectuals.
Which is to say that despite
living in this silly part of the
world, I enjoy brooding and
thinking, which is why
I love existentialism.

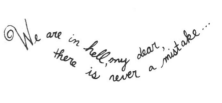
We are in hell, my dear, there is never a mistake...

Every day, Moose brings up topics that lead to enlightening discussions.

If life has no meaning, why bother with homework?

Why? Anyone?

Hollis?

Because there are consequences to everything we do. Sartre says that we aren't subject to fate. That you make decisions based on who you are. But the real question is....

How do you actually know who you are?

This was Hollis McAdams. Everyone was impressed with Hollis's answer. Me included, I admit.

Hollis McAdams has a father who is quite rich. He moved to Monterey last year and is even friends with Clint Eastwood. Hollis didn't want to go, so she lives here with her half-sister. Though she hangs out with ditzy popular girls like Ava, Lake, and Torrey, I know she is smart because super-intense guys like Noah, the newspaper editor, have crushes on her. Last year, Reza had a crush on her as well. Oh, he wouldn't admit it. But he got obsessed with psychoanalyzing her. He had read some book by a guy named Malcolm Gladwell and said that Hollis was a "connecter." She was able to branch out.

It didn't mean that she was nice. But it did mean she was curious.

Hollis McAdams and I have free period together.

(A thoroughly brilliant invention, by the way.)

Initially, we would do our homework separately. We would never have said a word to each other besides "hi," but existentialism was changing everything. By the time the week was over, we were not doing home-work at all.

More importantly....

As it turns out, during our very free period, Neil is doing a faculty study with Mrs. Hannity, the art teacher. He skates past us carrying weird arty stuff from the upper school Art Barn to the middle school studio. Our bench is conveniently located between the two.

I'd like to point out that over the past week, he has stopped by **four** times. And you know what he said to me yesterday?

Its quite obvious, Sartre, that — like you and me and Reza and Hollis — Neil has an intellect. He talks about things that are important, like grandmothers. What sort of a boy values his grandmother and talks of her fondly?!? Only an interesting one!

Which brings me to the biggest, most important thing that I discovered this week. On Friday, while walking across the parking lot to wait for my mother to pick me up, something very very interesting popped out of nowhere.

Neil's girlfriend, Ava Petropoulos, daughter of sporting goods magnate George Petropoulos... Ava Petropoulos, whose knowledge of her Greek heritage is limited only to the sorority system of the PAC 12 schools....

...was making out with Brett Dyson.

So it seems, Sartre, a ray of sunlight may actually be leaking into my miserable little Post Alex Epoch life. Here, as I sit on my bench of existential solitude and think about how to **be** and how death is final and random and that there is no god and that life is daft, desperate, and disenchanting, there may very well...

...be a chance for me.

ENGLISH 1 HONORS:
Existentialism Semester Project

February 19

The Mysterious and Heavenly Expanse

My dear Jean-Paul Sartre,

Now, let's not get all carried away with this Neil Strumminger business. All the hi-and-bye back and forth over the past week hasn't **exactly** led to a request for my hand in marriage.

However. I got some good advice this weekend from Urvashi Auntie, my mom's friend from Bombay who has been our houseguest for the past few days. There's absolutely no one on earth who gets these vague, who-are-you-type-Mr.-Moosewood questions better than Urvashi Auntie.

Now, Urvashi Auntie is my favorite Auntie. She and my mom have known each other since they were ten when they went to the Convent of Jesus and Mary together in Bombay. My mom says that she's an "armchair intel-lectual" and these days they are really different. My mom married my dad and moved to America and is a housewife. Urvashi Auntie married an Indian guy and then divorced him and then married another Indian guy and divorced **him** and then she married an Englishman who she loved a lot named William. He worked for a place called the "World Bank..."

...until he died last year. But I like Urvashi Auntie.

We have an understanding.

Urvashi Auntie talked and talked and talked...about how she used to be a model for a sari company and how she had an affair with some famous painter and then she talked about her family home and the traffic in Mumbai and all the old places where she and my mom used to hang out and smoke cigarettes and talk about intellectual things. She talked about how she was an atheist and my mom was an atheist only because they had to go to a **terrible** convent school that would make atheists out of the most devout little Hindus. And she talked about how she missed London and how she missed her dead husband and how his untimely demise had left her with three quarrelsome and greedy step-children who were trying to **nip** her out of his will.

I'm no expert in the matter, but I think she was a teensy bit drunk....

When I woke up the next morning,
this note was on my bed.

Dearest Tina,

You may think I wasn't paying attention, but I was. To explain to you what a mysterious expanse is, I want to tell you the following story.

When Krishna was a small baby, he used to do naughty things. One day, his mother found him lolling about in the forest and he was dirty as hell. She bent down to wipe his mouth. But as she did so, something very strange happened. She peered inside his mouth and before her lay THE ENTIRE UNIVERSE. She saw herself in there, in her little village in Gujarat, cleaning the mouth of her son and then MANY MORE UNIVERSES inside his mouth and so on so forth.

This story illustrates what I meant yesterday, though mostly it is interpreted by total idiots. My interpretation goes as follows and it is the best one.

1. People will tell you all sorts of things.
2. Don't listen to them.
3. Do as you please, but on one condition.
4. Know that there is a universe inside yourself.
5. And examine it.

This may seem compicated, but really it is not. Come visit me here in Bombay, darling, but don't call it Mumbai as that name was given to the city by a bunch of raving mad right-wing lunatics.

Red Hot Kisses.

Your fond,

Urvashi Auntie

ENGLISH 1 HONORS:
Existentialism Semester Project

March 5

A Perfectly Normal Tale

♥ Mon ami, Jean-Paul Sartre,

The teachers at Yarborough try to mitigate the amount of navel-gazing we indulge in by making students do socially responsible things like community service and charitable fundraisers. One such event is the "Valentine's Day Carnation Give-a-Thon." Students buy carnations to give to other students and the money goes to charity.

Personally, I don't think this carnation business is socially responsible at all because Valentine's Day is bad enough as it is without the stress of having to see if your name is called during geometry class for a carnation. The popular girls go nuts over these stupid carnations.

Last year, Alex and I sent one to each other and that's what I received: one carnation. So this year, I didn't expect to receive any. But I did.

This was the note that came with it and it was written on revolting scented paper.

Hi Tina,

I'm looking forward to working together.

Ted

Who is Ted, you ask?

Well. It all started Monday morning when the cast list was posted up on the wall of Mr. Moosewood's office.

I, **Tina M.**, am the lead in Mr. Moosewood's winter production of Rashomon, the biggest play of the year!

Su Ming got in too. Clearly, it had been Moose's master plan to get me off my bench of existential solitude, albeit by pasting me to these weirdos.

But even Neil said something about it during free period.

Indeed there is nothing like busyness to make your existential solitude fade a bit.

Suddenly, I've found that my life has become a hectic combination of schoolwork, lunchtime activities, and rehearsal.

For our first rehearsal, Mr. Moosewood bought us a bunch of kimonos from Japantown. He said that it would get us into the mood of the play.

We started by learning about Japan.

Japan this Japan that

Then we did a bunch of drama exercises and got acquainted with "method acting."

And then we did a read-through.

One thousand years ago in the ancient city of Kyoto...

The story began as a perfectly normal tale about a samurai and his wife going for a pleasant walk through the forest. Then a bandit comes out and kidnaps them.

That's when things get dicey. Actually, they get dicey on page 21.

p. 21

Holding her **writhing** body, his **mouth** seeks hers.

As it turns out, the bandit in this horrifying little play rapes the wife. Then four people who witnessed the crime give their own version of the story, the point being that the **truth is difficult to discern.**

The worst part was that there were to be several mouth-to-mouth kisses between my character and the bandit.

hot!

woo hoo!

yow!

Guys, please.

And **who** was playing this said bandit?

Yes, Ted. Ted Fresh, the very same fellow who gave me the carnation.

This may not seem Gandhi-esque or fair or good in the way my mother would want me to be, but Ted Fresh is **revolting.**

For the following reasons:

1. He eats fried fish sandwiches from vending machines and has notoriously bad breath.
2. He wears a stupid gothic raincoat (circa 1991).
3. He listens endlessly to that Eurotrash band Telefon.
4. He wears aviator sunglasses that he doesn't deserve (enraging), and
5. He once asked Lake to marry him in front of the entire upper school assembly. (She said no.)

If I were to choose who would be the worst person in the world to be fake raped by on a stage in front of everyone including my parents and probably Pinky Auntie, **IT WOULD BE TED.**

Just so you know, Mr. Moosewood, in case you open my sealed existential diary, I think this play is a terrible choice. I think you should have chosen **Xanadu.**

And why Su Ming has a fondness for Ted, I cannot understand.

Since this is my existential diary, I suppose I should be very, very truthful ("**A taste for truth at any cost is a passion which spares nothing.**" — Albert Camus, your rival and I'm sorry to bring him up but Moose put this quote on the board yesterday and I find it rather succinct).

Maybe I should tell you something you already suspect.

With the exception of eighth grade spin-the-bottle, I have not kissed **anyone**. Yes, I know. PATHETIQUE. In some parts of the world, it is not that pathetique. But here, in this part of the world, it is. I may very well be the only person my age in the whole of the southern coast of California, in this den of bucolic iniquity and transcendental meditation and Mr. Zog's Sex Wax, who hasn't kissed a boy. This, Monsieur Sartre, is pathetique.

So, this is just to say that after all this time waiting, I would have to avoid the kiss altogether. There was no way that Ted Fresh was going to be my first kiss. No. Freaking. Way.

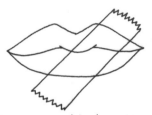

And I would certainly not encourage him by acknowledging receipt of that dastardly carnation.

Which brings me to the worst moment of the week. And it was AFTER the reading.

I had walked into the bathroom to change out of my kimono when I heard some voices in the stalls and realized they belonged to Alex and Claudia.

Oh, and I saw Tina with Neil during her freeper.

Yeah, she's had a crush on him forever.

Can you believe this? Alex had told Claudia I had a crush on Neil. But, worse, do you know what that myopic louche said?

Like she has a chance. That's what she said. I waited till they were gone and left the bathroom without even changing.

ENGLISH 1 HONORS:
Existentialism Semester Project

March 22

Things Can Change in a Day

Well, my dear fellow,

Two weeks have passed since my last entry, Sartre, and I just re-read it and I have this to say: Hah! Gotcha! If you have been concerned for my well-being and my experience or lack thereof — **WORRY NO MORE.**

After the bathroom conversation, I was done with Alex. She and her group could turn into a four-headed monster for all I cared. I was working on my **personal existential identity.**

These days, Hollis and I pretty much talk the whole time during freeper.

Every day, Neil comes and talks to us and the truth has been confirmed: Ava dumped Neil for Brett Dyson. It isn't weird anymore that Neil and I talk all the time. And Reza was right. Hollis is much more interesting than Lake or Ava or other popular girls who are always laughing and whispering about something. (God knows what popular girls laugh about, Sartre, but they are always laughing.) Hollis seems above it.

And when you're branching out, you need an ally.

Everyone in Moose's class had to pick an existentialism project. For example, Jeff Whitacre is shooting the inside of other people's closets.

> Vile.

And, somehow, Lake got roped into making detailed notes of all her family's garbage.

Hollis's project was to go around to different religious places to learn about people's religions. "See where morality comes from" is what Moose told her. Here are some of the people she interviewed.

A monk   A Hasid   A priest   A Mormon   A shaman   A Jew for Jesus

She's been really into it.

> I've never felt so peaceful. It's like a psychic clearing-house.

I know what she means, is what I told her. That said, I'm not totally sure I do.

Last week, she even went to the Hare Krishna temple on Venice Blvd.

> What made you join the brotherhood?

Anyways, Hollis's life is quite different from mine. In addition to living with her half-sister, she also lives with her half-sister's boyfriend, who she refers to as Nookie. Hollis has a boyfriend too, an older guy. Older than college, even. My parents would be in my business in a simply legendary way if I had a boyfriend. Forget about if he was older than college.

Speaking of religion...yesterday, Neil asked me if I could tell him about Buddhism. Now, obviously, I know nothing about Buddhism because my mom says she's an atheist. But I was hardly going to **say** that...

...so, I faked my way through it pretty well. Actually, we talked for so long that Mrs. Hannity came looking for him.

As soon as he left, Hollis and I had this conversation.

Whatever happened to you and Alex? You used to be inseparable. Now she's, like, pasted to Eric.

Seriously.

Lame. I can't believe she dropped your friendship because she got a boyfriend. That's, like, fifth grade.

I know.

I know what we need to do. We need to find **you** a boyfriend.

I mean, don't you have a little crush on Neil?

What??

Come on. Your face changes when he's around! Who cares? Why don't you tell me. Maybe I can **help** you?

You do have a crush on him.

This, of course, led me to wonder....

Whatever did she mean?

Well.

Popular girls seem to know a thing or two about how to do things. Or maybe it was just Hollis. Maybe Hollis was truly gifted because at 8:30 am the following morning (today) in the location of Yarborough Academy, California, America, the World, the Universe, a little cupid work was indeed done and **THIS IS WHAT HAPPENED.**

Well. Good. God.

Dearest **dear** Jean-Paul Sartre,

This little bit of news, as you can imagine, is quite an enormous step forward and its occurrence, my dear, dead existential philosopher, has led me to **three** epiphanies!!!

Epiphany #1

What have I been doing for the past six years spending all my time skulking around and playing games with Alex Imogene Leach. **Childish!**

Epiphany #2

Popular people like Hollis are way more interesting. Maybe that's why they're popular! Who needs a revolution? Look at Alex and her wannabee Sylvia Plath study group. Singing songs and writing depressing poetry and obsessing over their boyfriends. Its waaaay more fun to sit around and talk about philosophy and hear stories about Clint Eastwood and step-mothers and older men. Duh!

Epiphany #3

I am not going to sit on the fringes of hell, like all those unhappy freaks of **No Exit,** in their claustrophobic hotel room of death. Mon dieu. I don't want to be an observer, skulking about on the edges of society with a delinquent ex-Mormon. It may have seemed fun at the time but not any-more!!! I'm taking action and today's events are proof that I might even get some experience. Indeed, I can have the cute surfer boyfriend of my dreams. Even my sister had a boyfriend by my age. He was a German exchange student named Leopold and he was actually a senior. But my sister has never had any sort of problem with action or experience. The point is, without doing things, I will end up in your hotel room from hell, having lived a life like that Miss Havisham character. Except I'll be this little old Indian lady living in some tract home in Newport Beach.

Thank god for you, Jean-Paul Sartre, my grim old grand-pere.

Thanks to you, I'm improving my existence! No **wonder** you're a freaking genius!

For the past few days, I have been spaced out. I've had a million random thoughts about the **very nature of existence.**

Like why do butterflies live for a day??

And what's beyond outer space?

What is the history of toothpaste and exclamation points??

Why is the sky blue when it is only a reflection of **water?**

Why are humans the only animals who cry??

What is happening in Nairobi, Kenya, when I am sitting in geometry?

And, **most of all,** what will I wear to the spring formal?????

Wake up, Tina. It's your line.

I have to say, aside from Ted Fresh and the weird subculture of the drama geeks, I actually love being in a play. It's **fun** to be someone else!

All in all, everything seemed to be going much better. Even without Alex. **Especially** without Alex. I was the lead in the play. I was going biking with Neil Strumminger, the boy of my dreams, and I might even win an Oscar one day.

Of course, there was the scene with Ted.

Mr. Moosewood, being a wise sort of man, must have known that kissing Ted was going to be terrible even for the most worldly and tolerant of people because we had always just skipped the kissing part. Moose would just say "yes, yes," and we'd move on. But now we had started blocking and moving around the stage.

The thing is, even during the lead up, I could tell something was different.

What I realized very quickly was that Ted, who's not exactly Marlon Brando, was going all the way with this whole method business.

And, very quickly, we were in a real battle of sorts.

Distracted by his grunts and pokes and yelping, I completely forgot to grit my teeth. So, when it came to the kiss, he just grabbed me and plunged his bacteria-covered idiot savant tongue...

...into my mouth...

...and held it there for a good, long while.

And **you**, Mr. Jean-Paul Sartre?

What was your first kiss?

BECAUSE THAT WAS MINE.

Now, I am a feminist, but not too much of one. So it wasn't like I was going to go on and on about patriarchical violation like my sister would have, even though that's **precisely** what was going on.

I just sat around on **another** bench of existential solitude, this one in the quad, thoroughly pitying myself. Thoroughly **pissed** off at Ted for hijacking my plans.

Thoroughly **grateful** I had a real boyfriend coming. Hopefully. Maybe. Eventually. Saturday.

My first kiss. A fact that no one will ever know. **Ever.**

ENGLISH 1 HONORS:
Existentialism Semester Project

April 2

The Mysterious and Heavenly Expanse, Part 2

Dear Jean-Paul Sartre,

My brother, Rahul, is a lover not a fighter. And the reason I know this is because after his college girlfriend Suzie broke his heart, he cried his eyes out for six months straight.

But after six months were over, he felt better and realized he was lonely.

Girlfriends were too much trouble.

Having been a spectacular hit on the dating website he joined some months back, he began whittling down offers from Indian girls from all over the world.

And that's how he met

They seemed like a strange match to me, but I'm not the one who wanted a wife.

Anyways, they started going out.

And my mom and Pinky Auntie went crazy.

A few months later, by virtue of some positive thinking and a bunch of frequent flier miles, Rahul got engaged to Rani.

Which would have been fine except that after all the phone calls were made and an engagement party was planned and a wedding date set, my calm, predictable brother did something that no one could predict:

He freaked out.

Not like anyone was asking me, but I could see this coming a mile away.

I don't know if panic attacks were all the rage back when you were alive in France, but they're common parlance in these parts. You can always find someone in any random group who's had one. My dad, the doctor, said that Rahul maybe should take some panic pills, but Rahul said no — to his credit — because Rahul's problem can't be solved with a pill. DUH! His problem is way more vague.

My parents had an arranged marriage as that is the custom among the people of India. But before you get all worked up and into a tizzy and act all shocked, I just want to let you know that it's not like they showed up on their wedding day with leaves on their faces and stood before a priest. They actually dated.

Oh, they bicker now and then...

But mostly they seem happy.

In any case, the following conversation hardly surprised me.

Are you missing the feeling of being in love? Or the feeling of love?

?

You have to believe it is going to work.

Being in love is a temporary emotion.

There is a practical element to love, Rahul.

Can you believe this?

Where are **you** going?

I am going biking.

Wear your helmet.

What are they talking about?

As for me, I have a different view on these matters.

Love should be practical?

There was going to be nothing practical whatsoever about my no-home-work-weekend leisure activities with Neil Strumminger! SUCH is my commitment to practicality.

124

There he went again. With all the religious stuff. I had some vague idea that nirvana had something to do with love and the universe and some kind of New Age nonsense that Mr. Moosewood would probably love. Or that it was something like that mysterious expanse Urvashi Auntie was talking about. I didn't know.

What I **did** know was that all of his **talk** was getting us **nowhere** as far as **kissing** was concerned.

It turns out it was a *genius* answer.

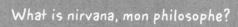
What is nirvana, mon philosophe?

It is....

....a kiss.

And aside from one moment that was a tiny bit awkward...

It was the most magical day ever.

Rahul, you can't marry Rani if you're not in **love!**

I tried to tell my mom and sister about Neil Young....

What could they possibly understand? Even my sister. Roped in by societal deception as they are.

Thank god for you, Sartre, you're the only one I have.

Only love can break your heart. A greater truth I have **never** heard.

Dearest *dear* Jean-Paul Sartre...

I am in *Love*

My Existential Diary

And my conclusion is:

Love Is the Best Feeling Ever.

I want to be in love forever! I **need** to be in love forever. I must **forever be in love**! Being in love is love! What could be more real than this. And you would agree, you being the sort who was a success with the ladies, even if one of them was a lesbian.

Being in love makes everything different. First of all, it makes you happy for no apparent reason!

It also makes you nice to people like Mr. Spencer at the community service convalescent home.

And love makes you want to spread all sorts of goodwill.

Love makes you feel powerful! It makes you want to fight the bad guys.

SLAP!

WHAP!

Like Ted.

Who tried to French kiss me again.

Quit sticking your tongue into my mouth.

What are you talking about?

LIAR!!!
And if you do it again, I will BITE YOUR TONGUE OFF.

?

I admit that it may not have been the most Gandhi-esque way of dealing with the situation, but it certainly was effective. I would have thought that Mr. Moosewood being so enlightened and all would have understood something like patriarchical violation.

There are other ways to deal with these kinds of things, Tina.

Whatever, colonizer.

But I guess not.

When I saw Neil on Monday morning, I felt something flutter in not just my stomach, but other parts of my body as well. I don't understand why everyone isn't in love with Neil! Next time, I was definitely going to let him stick his hand up my shirt. Next time....

What is love?

The definition is as clear as a blue sky in January.

I wanted to tell Alex that I had experience. I had felt it too — and not with some gummy banshee like Eric! And he was probably even going to be my boyfriend. I was going to crack Neil open and tell him everything. I wanted to comb through our conversations for clues into his soul.

I'm not one of those girls who falls for new-age poppycock, but I feel like I am **one** with Neil. In fact, I am one with the universe. I am one with a...

But enough of the drama.

Winter has turned to spring.

SIX
PISTOLS

And I am feeling good.

ENGLISH 1 HONORS:
Existentialism Semester Project

April 10

How the Matchmaker Intervened

Dear Jean-Paul Sartre,

You may not believe it, but here in Southern California there actually is a difference between the seasons. No, it's not as extreme as in other places and, yes, everyone freaks out when it rains for more than two hours, and they put on their favorite jungle rainforest attire. But these days there is no rain! Why? Because in California it rains in winter, silly, and it's spring that is in the air. Which means, my dear dead Frenchman, something you must well know: **love** is in the air.

Love was definitely in the air this weekend. Saturday morning, my mother was in a frenzy. The sort of frenzy that meant an important person was coming over.

When it came to saying exactly who was coming, she was cagey. Typical. So, I asked my dad.

This explained why Anjali was getting stoned in her room earlier.

After my sister Anjali graduated from architecture school, she worked at a firm in New York. On the side, she painted and made video installations. During this time, she had an architect boyfriend whose name was Juergen. They visited once and all they did was talk amongst themselves about totally vague things.

I went with them to see a building that was supposedly super-famous.

Obviously, Juergen is an idiot, not just for his bad taste, but because shortly thereafter he dumped my sister and broke her heart! Everything in New York seemed cold and full of bitter memories. Her job became unbearable. She even started to hate architecture.

So she came home to figure it out and did this in the following ways:

1. Crying.

2. Smoking copious amounts of weed.

3. And drinking lots of alcohol.

Things came to head, however, when Anjali went to her childhood friend Lolly's wedding.

This last debacle was a wee bit of a mistake because my mom got super-mad.

She gave Anjali a lecture on how feminism and being charitable were worthy, but saying what Lolly should and shouldn't do was unseemly for the occasion and that most of all it was **not** okay to get inappropriately drunk at a wedding.

It turns out that Pinky Auntie saw the whole mess and decided it was high time to rein Anjali in by getting her married off.

She had a nephew who was handsome and highly eligible.

So Pinky Auntie had a word with my mom who had a word with Anjali, whose mood had vastly improved because she had gotten accepted to an art colony and also got a job working for a video installation artist named "Detroit." One word. Like Madonna.

Anjali complained.

But she didn't really have a choice in the matter.

A few days later, Anjali put some towels under the door and toked up.

I have to say that if **my** suitable girl arrived stoned, I would probably be just a little peeved.

However, it became pretty obvious pretty quickly that Anjali and Rohit were probably not suitable for each other at all.

Pinky Auntie had also brought along her other nephew, Aditya. He was nineteen and studying animation at a place called Cal Arts.

Aditya's another arty type, but Rohit's a **DOCTOR!**

Tina, go hang out with Aditya. He seems nice and he's closer to your age.

N.O.

The thing is, Pinky Auntie had done such a good job of pasting Anjali and Rohit together that Aditya didn't have anyone to talk to. So, he started eavesdropping on **their** conversation as Anjali was trying to explain what this video installation guy Detroit was trying to do.

?

The open luggage conveys a feeling of exile —

Exiled in an airport?

Metaphysical exile.

Er, is there money in video installing?

But **then:**

Are you talking about "Detroit"?

Why YES!

Ah, another arteeste!

You're his **ASSISTANT?**

As it turned out, this peculiar artist that my sister was going to be working for, the one that maybe two people in the world knew about, was some kind of a god to a really small group of people and this fellow Aditya was part of that group!

And so, for the rest of the evening, even though Pinky Auntie tried valiantly to pry them apart, Anjali and Aditya came to some hard and fast conclusions.

Of course, Pinky Auntie was horrified because it was probably against the matchmaker's handbook to set someone up with a guy who was five years younger — nineteen years old, technically a teenager, which is a little disturbing.

But, then again, I kind of wonder about what's inside Pinky Auntie's matchmaker handbook in the first place.

Of course, there was a fuss over what happened. My guess is that my mom is starting to wise up to the smell of weed, the so-called artistic melancholia, and the dating of minors. It's only a matter of time before she lays down the law, if you want to know what I think.

But, until then, love will prevail.

As for my dad, he'd had a few whiskeys. And whenever he's had a few whiskeys he starts to quote Hamlet.

To thine own self be true.

Which I thought was kind of sappy and probably true. The only thing is:

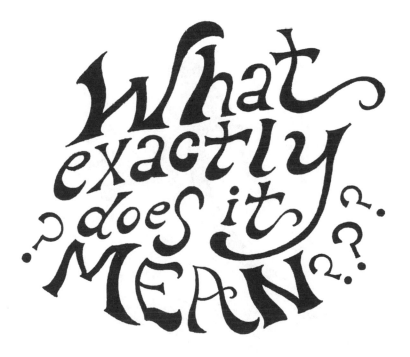

ENGLISH 1 HONORS:
Existentialism Semester Project

April 24

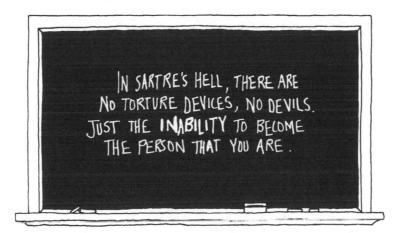

IN SARTRE'S HELL, THERE ARE
NO TORTURE DEVICES, NO DEVILS.
JUST THE **INABILITY** TO BECOME
THE PERSON THAT YOU ARE.

Sartre's Hell

These words, Sartre, were written on the blackboard today by Mr. Moosewood with regard to our in-class discussion of your book, **No Exit**, and I have a bone to pick with you.

"...the inability to become the person that you are." That YOU are. The word "you" is **second person singular**, Sartre, and that's where my problem lies.

I am not one thing.

I will **never** be one thing.

I am east, west, happy, sad, normal, freakish, plain, pretty, Indian, American, and quite possibly a touch of Greek due to Alexander the Great's invasion of the Punjab Province in 327 B.C. I live in California, but someday it might be Zanzibar or the Left Bank of Paris. Maybe the right. I have no idea. **Do you see how complicated it gets?**

It has been some weeks since love was in the air. And I have to say, things are not going smoothly.

First of all, there was this:

My dad has long foregone any dreams of me going to Harvard or Yale or Columbia or medical school or being brilliant like my brother or sister. But the C- was too much, and he told me I needed to stop doing my many extracurriculars.

The truth is: he's right. **I am distracted these days.**

Take play practice, for example.

The non-Gandhian method of boxing Ted's ears and publicly humiliating him has proven to be highly effective in that he hasn't tried to French kiss me again. But I was kind of feeling bad about the whole thing — you know, calling him out on patriarchical violation.

Two days ago, Su Ming was unavailable for lunch, so I walked to my old bench behind the elementary school and guess what I saw? Ted. Sitting on **my** bench of existential solitude. He was eating a sandwich and reading Dostoevsky for Mrs. Halperin's A.P. Russian Literature course.

It's shocking to think that I'm more like Ted than I thought.

There is a much bigger problem, however.

It has been three weeks since my date with Neil, and in case you haven't noticed, we're not exactly boyfriend and girlfriend. Or even friends.

Which is really frustrating because I think about him all the time.

And I pray...

Frankly, I am a total mess.

He should call you again, don't you think? Or at least invite you to lunch.

Or at least talk to you.

Oh, I have tried to explain to Su Ming that I wouldn't want to eat lunch with all those stupid popular girls, but she doesn't get these kinds of things. She doesn't have any experience. She doesn't understand that love hurts. Not everyone gets to have love just fall into their laps. I reminded her that there were many instances when Neil had talked to me.

1. Like when he told Willie Sharpe about our bike ride the other day.

2. Or when he came up to me from behind and tickled me at my locker.

3. Or that he would sometimes come around to me and Su Ming's bench at lunch.

4. And that he would always yell my name when he skated by my locker.

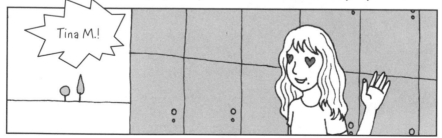

But then he was off. Where was he going anyways?

I have had no choice, Sartre, but to become:

Tina M.

"STALKER."

As I continue acting in Moose's spring play it has become increasingly obvious to me that there are connections to be made between this alleged masterpiece, Rashomon, and my own life, and that the person who wrote this story must have been pretty smart and maybe even a genius.

There are, indeed, different but plausible versions of the truth.

Confusing Truth #1:

Take Alex, for example.

I had been watching Alex of late. She was still hanging on to Eric. But something was also a little different.

She seemed to have the tiniest bit of air around her.

And then I overheard a conversation between Claudia and Alex.

BLECH!

That **ghastly**, bespectacled **viper** who stole **my best friend's soul!**

A few months ago, Alex would have laughed at advice like that.

Had she changed that much? Is she who she was BEFORE? Or is she who she is NOW?

BEFORE   NOW

NERDY AND SMART   SLUTTY AND STUPID!!!!!!!

Which one was the truth?

And, of course, there was Neil.

After our crazy, awesome bike ride, and after saying that he wanted to go on another crazy, awesome bike ride, I cannot understand why we **haven't gone out again.**

Three days after bike ride: **Five** days after bike ride:

Why would he never follow up?

Could it be that my version of our bike ride and his version of the bike ride were two different things altogether?

Which one was the truth?

Quite frankly, this business of love that was so fun a few weeks ago is not so exciting anymore.

Last week alone, I slipped up in Chem lab and added some weird substance to the Bunsen burner concoction, I forgot my lines during play practice, and left my history homework at home twice. The second time my mom came to school and dropped it off and she wasn't terribly pleased.

So, Jean:

It is I, Tina, writing to you — your little Hindu from Southern California. I **desperately** need some advice. I am indeed many things — east, west, happy, sad — but right now....

I am **LOVESICK**.

Yes, my dear dead grandfather of French philosophical thought, the highs
have swung to lows and I have fallen into something I am going to term
CEM or Chronic Existential Malaise. This disease, a modern one, as far as
I know, does not exist in the DSM manual, though I should say it has been
a while since I've flipped through. It is characterized by angst, anxiety,
loneliness, depression, and death.

Just yesterday, I overheard Lake say that Amy Baumgartner and Neil were going to the prom together, which was shocking to learn. But then I realized that he didn't seem to be going **out** with Amy. They weren't holding hands or being boyfriend-girlfriend or whatever it is people **do** when they're a couple. They were just going to prom.

Then this morning, things really got thrown into a tizzy when Neil told me a dream he had.

> I was swimming around Redondo when a school of sharks came up behind me.

There are no sharks in Redondo as far as I know and you don't want to swim there unless you want to get Hepatitis A. But it was a dream and that's what he was doing.

> And then I swam into one big mouth and it saved my life.

> A mouth?

> You know. Nirvana. Like you said. It made me think of you.

One moment of beauty in a cesspool of confusion. The time had come. I had to talk to someone popular about the Neil situation. It could no longer be just me and Su Ming.

There was only one person it could be.

To be honest, Hollis had started to take the Hare Krishna thing a bit too far. The other day, she showed up at school wearing a bindi and some necklaces she bought at the temple store!! But anyway, I told her my story — every little bit. I should have talked to her a long time ago. She was very helpful.

Drinking, pills. Everyone pretending to be cool. It would definitely be stupid.

Now, this was an interesting point.

I hadn't really thought of calling him. It was true.

Perhaps the problem was I simply hadn't been clear enough.

173

...was the first of **SIX GODDAMN TIMES.**

How was I supposed to know that there was something wrong with his phone and that it was going to keep hanging up on me in the middle of my sentence.

Now he knows the truth.

He finally called me back at 10 pm. Of course, I was in the shower.

Dude, there are, like, twenty messages from you on my phone, Tina. But it's totally completely fine, because my phone has been acting weird these days and Willie told me that it hung up on him a million times also. So, don't worry. Anyways...I'm just calling you to tell you that I ALREADY KNOW that you're coming to Lake's party because Ms. Hollis McAdams the first, or maybe the last, told me that she invited you and I hope you do so we can hang out and talk about our many mutual interests. I'll see you tomorrow during your freeper. Ciao.

Boys are an entirely unusual breed of human beings. Utterly incomprehensible and thoroughly annoying. I should never, **ever** fall in love again. What a terrible way to spend your time.

And then as Friday came, my **Chronic Existential Malaise** had morphed itself into something of a slightly different hue.

What to wear?!?

ENGLISH 1 HONORS:
Existentialism Semester Project

May 15

Horse Tranquilizer

I was dropped at Lake Bottomfelder's house at 9 pm by
Anjali and Aditya, who were now officially going out.

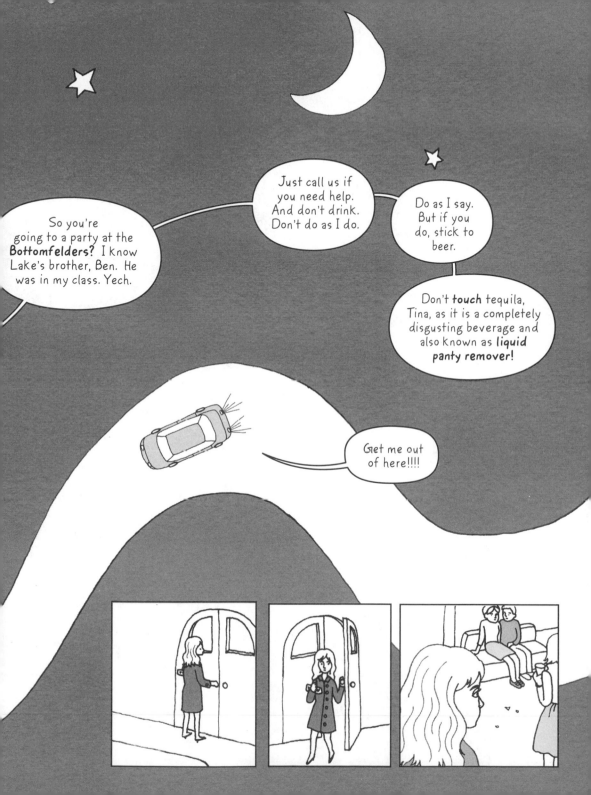

It was a large house with a lot of people in it.

184

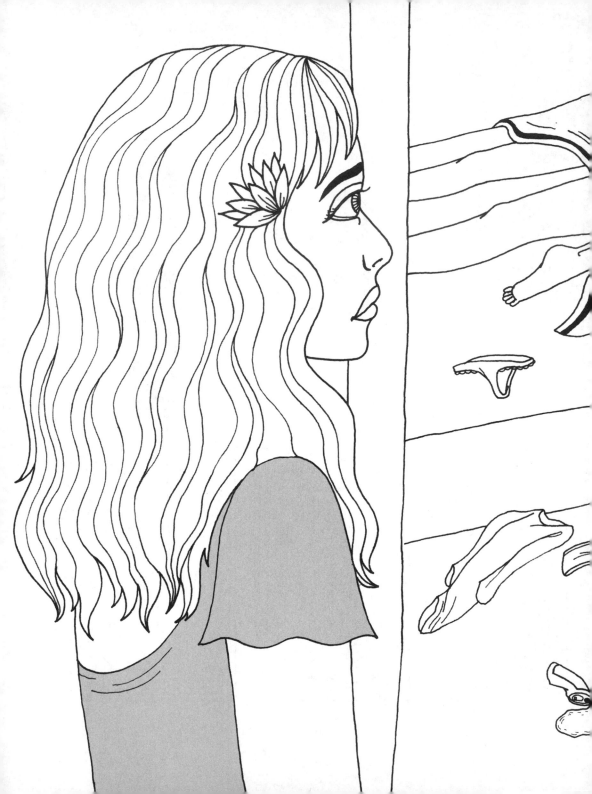

ENGLISH 1 HONORS:
Existentialism Semester Project

May 29

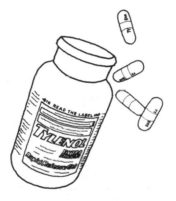

I Like You

Hi again, Jean-Paul Sartre,

I wish you'd warned me more explicitly, but maybe you did. Maybe it was in your book **No Exit** when you said that there was no mistaking hell. That we were all in hell. I guess things like this happen in the adult world all the time. I suppose that people you thought were good don't behave that way. But it is quite surprising who can let you down.

On Monday, everything was the usual. The popular people had more stories to talk about and laugh about. More inside jokes.

If Hollis was sorry about hooking up with Neil at Lake's party, she didn't show it.

In fact, she didn't say anything except to mumble a little something at the vending machine.

Then, like a puff of smoke, she disappeared from my life and became totally aloof. She would just sit there, far away, with her headphones on doing her homework.

As for Neil, I just avoided him. And he avoided me.

It seems, Sartre, that we are back to square one, you and I.

Su Ming's wrist had healed and she was back to practicing at least a few times a week. And I was alone, most days of the week. With a book.

Rashomon was to open the following weekend after Lake's party and we were rehearsing all the time. It was right before opening night, while I was getting ready in the makeup room, that I started to grasp that you could very well flit about like a little bug, staying busy, doing your homework and your extracurriculars and everything you're supposed to...

...and you could **still** end up in the hotel room of death, just like the characters in **No Exit.**

Being busy is different from taking action.

Opening night was sold out.

The music for the play was to be performed by a live trio and the pianist, of course, was Alex. Something was up with her. She was playing music with old-time fervor and wearing pre-Claudia attire. She kept staring at me and the truth was that I really didn't want her there.

So there we were on the stage, doing warm-ups, and the drama geeks were completely freaking out.

There was some-thing in the air, though. I realized that I needed to go for a walk and clear my head.

It seems that an endorphin rush is a funny thing and maybe I was indeed having one. Because for the past week while skulking around reading books and feeling bummed about the general bleakness of my sophomoric condition, I had not had the slightest desire to talk to Neil.

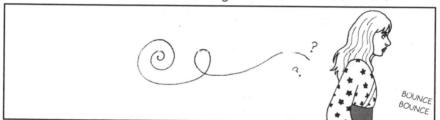

But right then, quite possibly while having this "endorphin" rush, I realized that there was nothing more I wanted to do than talk to him, which is why what happened next was both fortuitous and stomach lurching.

207

One general rule of thumb, Mr. Jean-Paul Sartre: when a boy you like does not like you back — at least not in the way you want him to — is that it's generally best not to start crying while wearing pancake-style make-up to make your debut as the lead in the school play five minutes before you go on. The one your parents are going to be attending and even your Pinky Auntie.

The second rule is that, if possible, it is best not to walk through the entire cast of aforementioned play and the audience members who have come to see it. It is particularly bad to walk past your ex–best friend under these circumstances with the aforementioned boy somewhere behind you.

Even Ted felt bad for me.

But I'll tell you something. When I got back to the makeup room, I felt one hundred times better.

And then...

That night, Rashomon was performed without a hitch.

We had three sold-out performances. People loved it. I was great and Ted wasn't bad either. We got a standing ovation on the third night and Mr. Moosewood's dreams of directing an opus magnum were fulfilled. It got a grand review in the Yarborough Academy Herald. Reza said he was impressed by my performance and brought me a flower. My parents came two nights in a row and everyone was thrilled. Even Pinky Auntie. It was a total hit.

Well done!

You were so good!

As for me, I've been told that I have great potential as an actress. But for now, I'm just happy the whole semester is done. And that this whole kiss business is behind me.

What monkey games that has been.

My mom had a conversation with Alex's mom during opening night and she has a serious foot-in-mouth disorder if you want to know the truth. Not only did she flat-out tell my mom that Eric broke up with Alex, she also started talking about her **virginity.**

So that's how I found out that Eric broke up with her.

On the final night, we had a cast party at Mr. Moosewood's faculty house. He played the video of the final performance and the drama geeks went nuts as if it were the most entertaining thing they'd ever seen in their lives.

Alex was at the party.

She might have done some work on her personal existential identity, is my guess. It's just a guess, though. And I can't say I was terribly enthused to see her. She's been rather a drip this semester, what with leaving me for old four-eyes and whatnot.

I can see she's feeling remorse over all her shenanigans, though she's still wearing some godawful outfits courtesy of her sudden and ill-conceived interest in fashion. When she'll go back to vintage Laura Ashley, I don't know. But if she thinks she can waltz back into my life — one, two, three, just like that — then she's sorely mistaken. That's just not going to happen.

Which brings me to....

ENGLISH 1 HONORS:
Existentialism Semester Project

June 12

The Plug-in Krishna

Dear Jean-Paul Sartre,

Well, it was inevitable. There had been signs before, early on, perhaps when Rahul's fiancée insisted on a pink-themed wedding at the Beverly Hills Hotel or when she said that she wanted to provide dermabrasion for the bridesmaids, that he had started to wonder. He's my brother, after all. He doesn't fall for that kind of malarkey.

Of course, the party had to be canceled. But worst of all, Rahul found himself in the throes of Chronic Existential Malaise. He should have been thrilled to get rid of that girl!

But that's just not how love works.

So that's when my sister and I cooked up an idea which is the best thing that I personally have ever heard of and I think you will agree, Mr. Jean Paul Sartre, because it's highly existential.

That way all the planning wouldn't go to waste and we could celebrate Rahul being disengaged! We took our brilliant idea to my mom and Pinky Auntie.

My sister valiantly tried to make the case when Pinky Auntie piped up.

So, after some thought and scaling back of the invite list, my mom decided to go ahead. We were to have a disengagement party, though we were forbidden to call it that. And it was really a celebration. Because soon after the wedding was canceled, I noticed that Rahul started going dancing with his friend Fernando. He got a puppy. And he seemed more engaged!

In fact, Sartre, it's quite possible that his Chronic Existential Malaise wasn't from his disengagement at all.

Maybe he's just gay.

And yesterday, finally, it was the last day of existentialism class. Everyone handed in their final papers and gave presentations. My favorite was Lake's. She had recorded her family's garbage for four full months and had this to say:

And Moose made his own announcement.

Reza told me the real reason for Mr. Moosewood's sabbatical. Apparently, Hollis's father got scared that Hollis was going to go join the Hare Krishnas, so he complained to Mr. Ackerman, our principal, about the existentialism class. Hollis's dad is one of the school's biggest donors, so it was kind of a big deal. Mr. Ackerman requested that Moose take a sabbatical.

Personally, I like Mr. Moosewood and all, but I don't know what he's doing at a stodgy old place like Yarborough.

As for Hollis, after Lake's party, I never had another proper conversation with her. I did see her crying one day in her car like the world was going to end. Then I heard some rumor that I actually believed. Her older boyfriend? You know how she met him?

He was her sister's 38-year-old boyfriend. The one she called Nookie.

Needless to say, that relationship ended. I think she is actually living at Lake's house now.

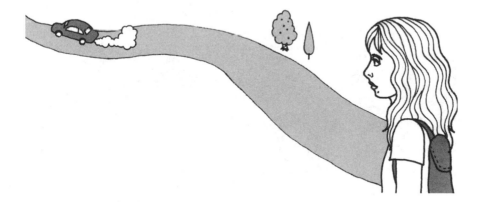

I don't think we'll ever be friends at Yarborough, but I have this feeling that one day, maybe years from now, maybe in a big city like New York, we'll meet for coffee in a cafe and talk about love, death, and god...

My mom picked me up from school yesterday and had an errand to run.

Cerritos is the Indian part of town. It's really not some colorful place like white people would love it to be, but a series of shops and restaurants just off the freeway. It's the most boring, ugly place on earth. I try to avoid going at all costs.

But, for some reason, today it was kind of fun.

Even though my mom says she's an atheist, she's cool with whatever I do. Which I think is probably existential of her.

225

Now that I have some experience, I think that Reza might be asking me out.

The great thing about summer is that it gets warm and everything becomes easier.

I got an A- on my math final.

Mrs. Abbott, the orchestra teacher, complimented my violin playing.

And Alex started to join Su Ming and me for lunch sometimes. Like today.

One day, maybe we'll talk about what happened this semester. But not today.

Today we'll just hang out.

On this bench.

And then it was time to be disengaged.

ENGLISH 1 HONORS:
Existentialism Semester Project

August 11

Epilogue

Dear Jean-Paul Sartre,

I've taken my own sweet time to finish off my diary. Mr. Moosewood has gone off to his monastery, so he's not going to care. It's been two months since the disengagement party.

I ran into Neil at the mall a few weeks ago and, can you believe it, we joked around. Funny how you can have all these feelings for someone and then they vanish and it's like they were never there to begin with. I'm lying. To be honest, I will always feel something. At least until he turns into a balding new-agey realtor in Redondo.

Aditya turned 20, and he and my sister are still going out. Even Pinky Auntie doesn't get a freaked-out look on her face about it any more. Personally, I think they're perfect for each other. Anjali's applying to graduate school in sculpting, so they can talk about all sorts of vague, irrelevant things for the rest of their lives as far as I'm concerned.

As for Alex, she and I are friends again, too. She had a fight with Claudia, which you can imagine is wholly unsurprising to me. We hang out, and she tried to explain where her head went during last semester and why she did the things she did. I understand. Love makes fools of us all. We're still different and the same, but maybe a little more different now, mainly because I've worked on my personal existential identity and so has she. Either way, I'm happy she's back in my life and with Su Ming we're a veritable picture of twenty-first-century ethnic enlightenment, let me tell you.

As for Reza, he and I continued our discussion of philosophy and politics all through the summer. He went to Iran and wrote me e-mails each week about what Tehran was like. Every other day for one month I got an e-mail from him! He wants to study international law at Harvard and maybe go back to Iran one day and help fight societal deception, which seems to exist a lot around there. Well, I told him, it exists everywhere, especially right here at Yarborough. In three years, I don't know where I'll be or what I'll be thinking. Wherever I am, I just hope I have a boyfriend. Or not. But if I do, I sort of hope that it's Reza.

So today, I am going to Yarborough for class registration. Eleventh grade starts in two weeks. I am taking chemistry, history, calculus, French, and my English Honors elective is Russian Literature. It's all Tolstoy and Chekhov for me, friend. I'll miss you, Sartre. I've enjoyed our one-sided exchange, and your image will hold a cherished spot next to my grandmother, my scarabee, and my plug-in baby Krishna....

...but **what exactly is existentialism**? I'm really not sure I understand.

I will say this:

As I pack up my diary to mail it to Mr. Moosewood, as I get ready to drive to school (I have my driver's license, by the way), as I prepare to face the throngs of bleached-out popular girls (they're going to be screaming all over the quad, I don't know what summer does to them), partiers, surfers, drama geeks, freakazoids, hippies, intellectuals, journalistic types, band people, and the people I know and the people I don't...I have learned one thing:

I think this is only the beginning.

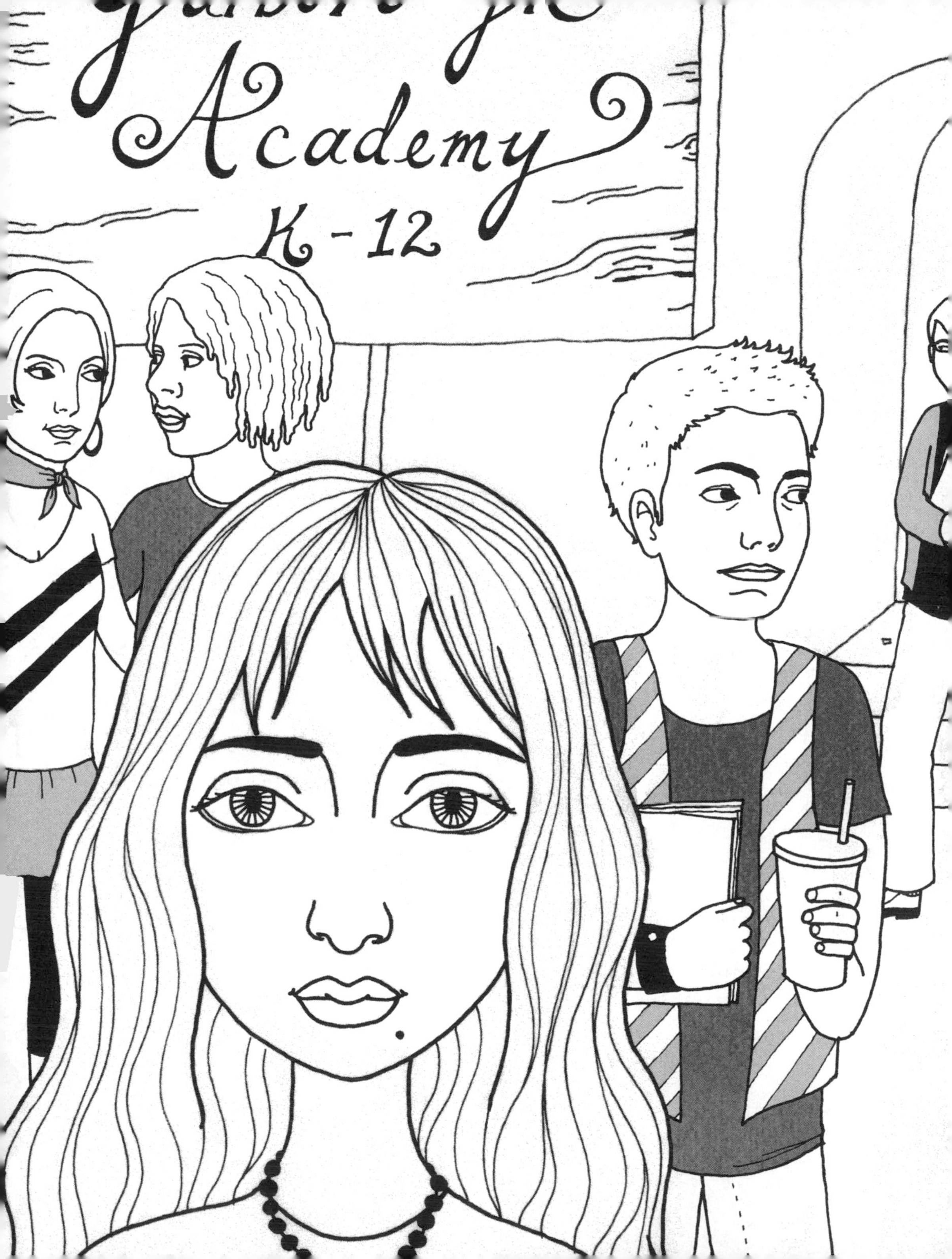
Academy
K-12

À bientôt, mon philosophe.

Tina M.

Acknowledgments

Putting this book together has been a labor of love, labor being the operative word but love running a close second. As such, there are a substantial number of people to thank. First off, Mari and I would like to thank our book designers, Bethany Powell and Christopher Moisan from Houghton Mifflin Harcourt, who have generously guided us in design and production issues from A to Z. We would also like to thank Ariadne Binderl, who provided continuous and abundant assistance throughout the production process and, most importantly, designed the type from my handwriting.

Mari would like to thank Steve Sueoka, Mark Todd, Esther Watson, and Mike Neumann. I would like to thank Zoe Ferraris, Deepak Nayar, Lisa Kohn, Dawn Mackeen, Raj Dhaka, Aldo Velasco, my two brothers — Ishaan Kashyap and Vikram Kashyap — as well as my beloved Cafe Orlin crew — Hilary Brougher, Maria Rosenblum, Jean-Christophe Castelli, and Samantha Davidson Greene. I'd also like to thank my cousin, Veena Vignale, who calmly — sometimes inadvertently — provided insight and feedback into the lifestyles of the modern teenager; and, of course, Jim Parkman who introduced me to existentialism at age fifteen and provided an adult primer on the matter.

In particular, I would like to thank Deanne Urmy and Anjali Singh, the two wise and brilliant editors who shepherded this project to fruition. Thank you for having faith in me and in us and in this book and for providing lucid insight from beginning to end. I'd also like to thank my remarkable agent, PJ Mark, for going through a zillion drafts with good humor, patience, and honesty. Finally, I'd like to thank my dear friend Varun Soni, without whom this never would have started, and, most of all, my parents, Moti and Suman Kashyap, without whom this never would have happened.

Die Camus # ♡